WHEN WE WENT TO THE ZOO

Jan Ormerod

WALKER BOOKS
LONDON

Ibex
Gibbons
Llama Rides
Pelicans
Elephants
Otters
Orang-Utans
Penguins
Sea-Lions
Toucans
Emus
Sharks
Tropical Fish
Boa Constrictors
Goats
Rabbits
Lions
Camel Rides
Giraffes
Grizzly Bears

When we went to the zoo, we saw

a gibbon swing across Gibbon Island.

The pelican yawned

as we rode past.

We sang, "Hi-de-hi-de-ho,

the elephant is so slow."

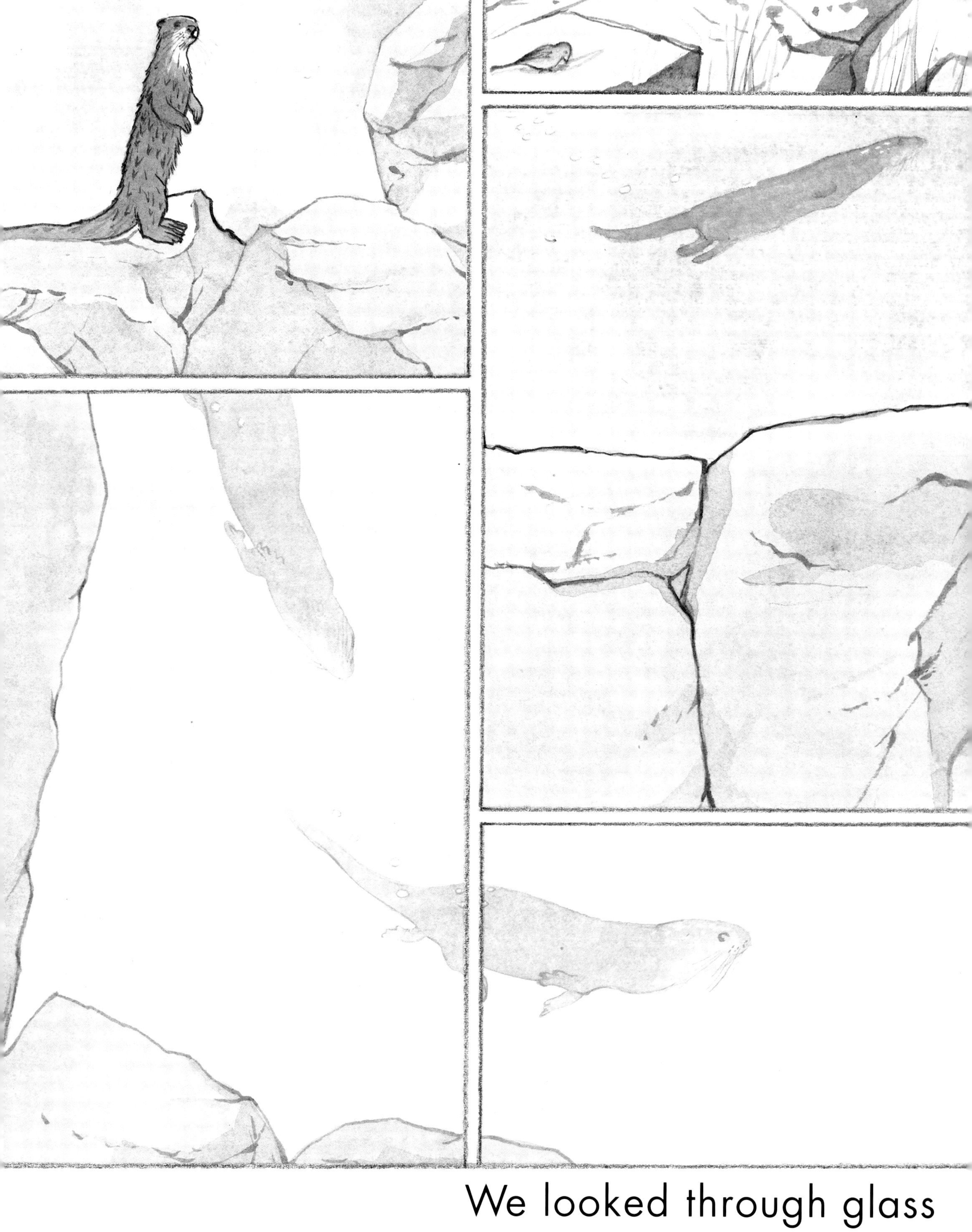

We looked through glass

and saw an otter underwater.

We saw an orang-utan carrying a

baby; another had a paper bag.

A penguin playing with a leaf

dived in and out of the water.

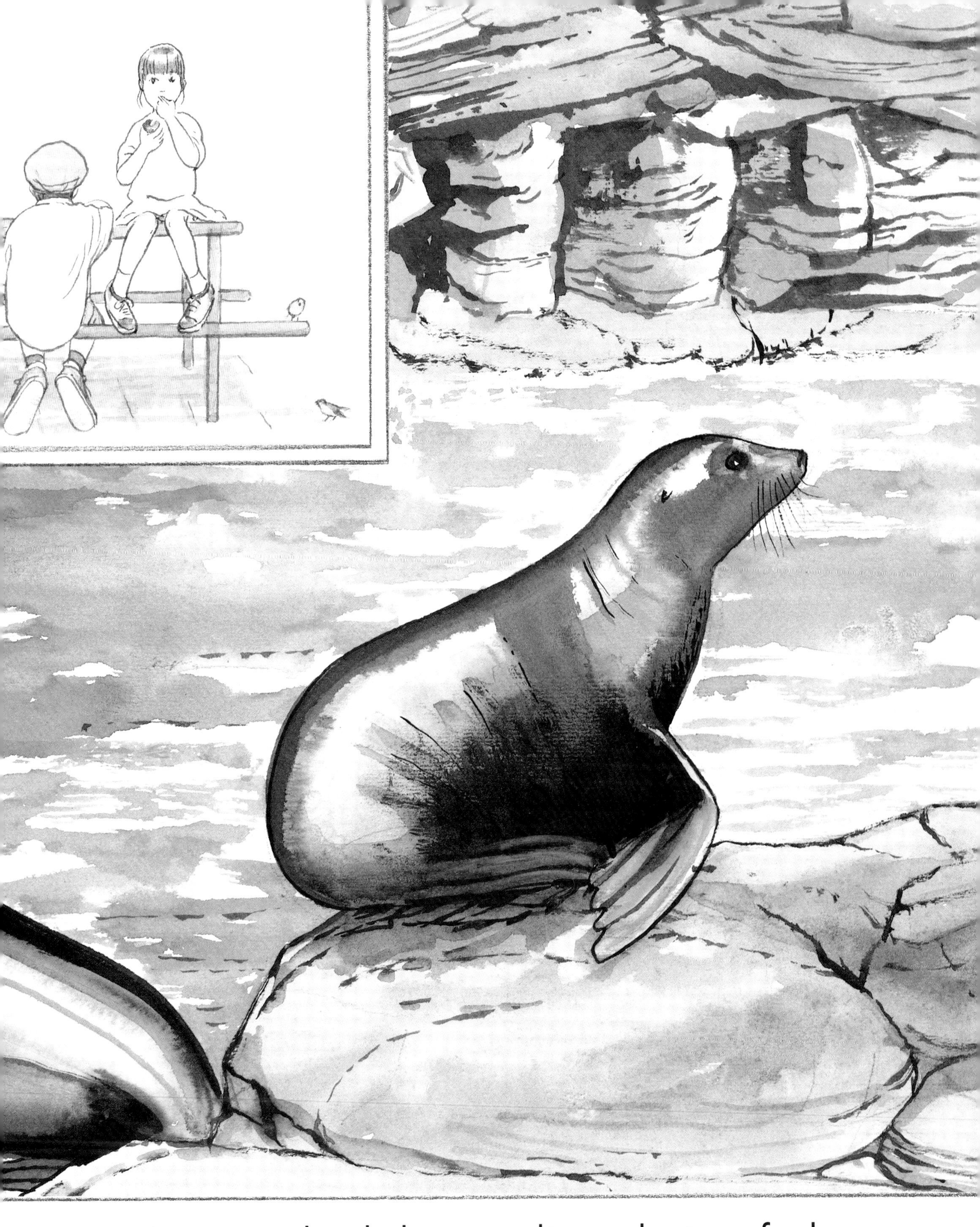

We watched the sea-lions being fed.

We saw two big-beaked toucans

and some stripy emu chicks.

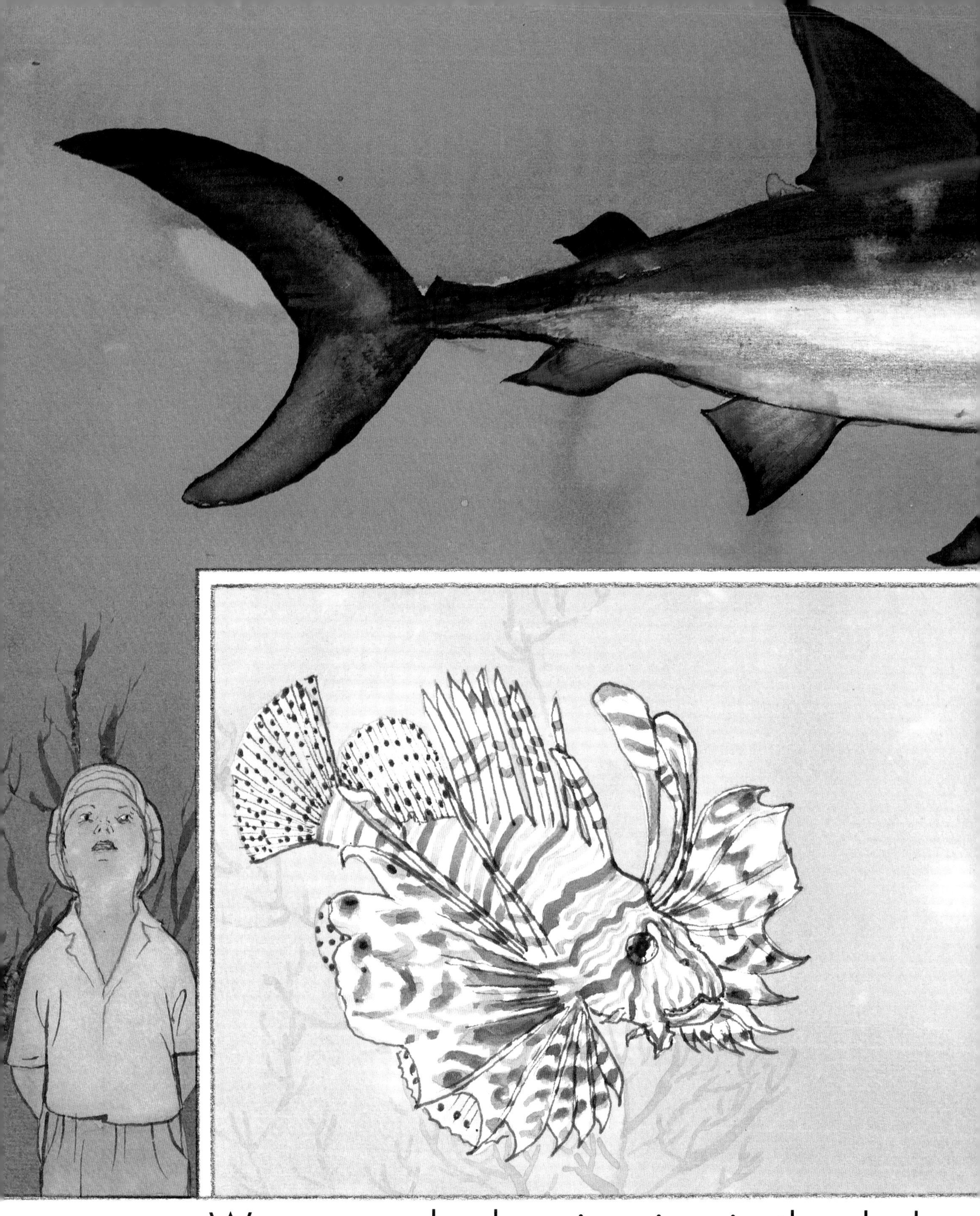

We saw a shark swimming in the dark,

and fish from a coral reef.

We touched a boa constrictor, a goat

and a rabbit, which was very soft.

We spent ages looking at a

lion, a lioness and their cubs.

We sang, "Bumpetty, bumpetty,

bump, we're on a camel's hump."

We saw the giraffes in their tall

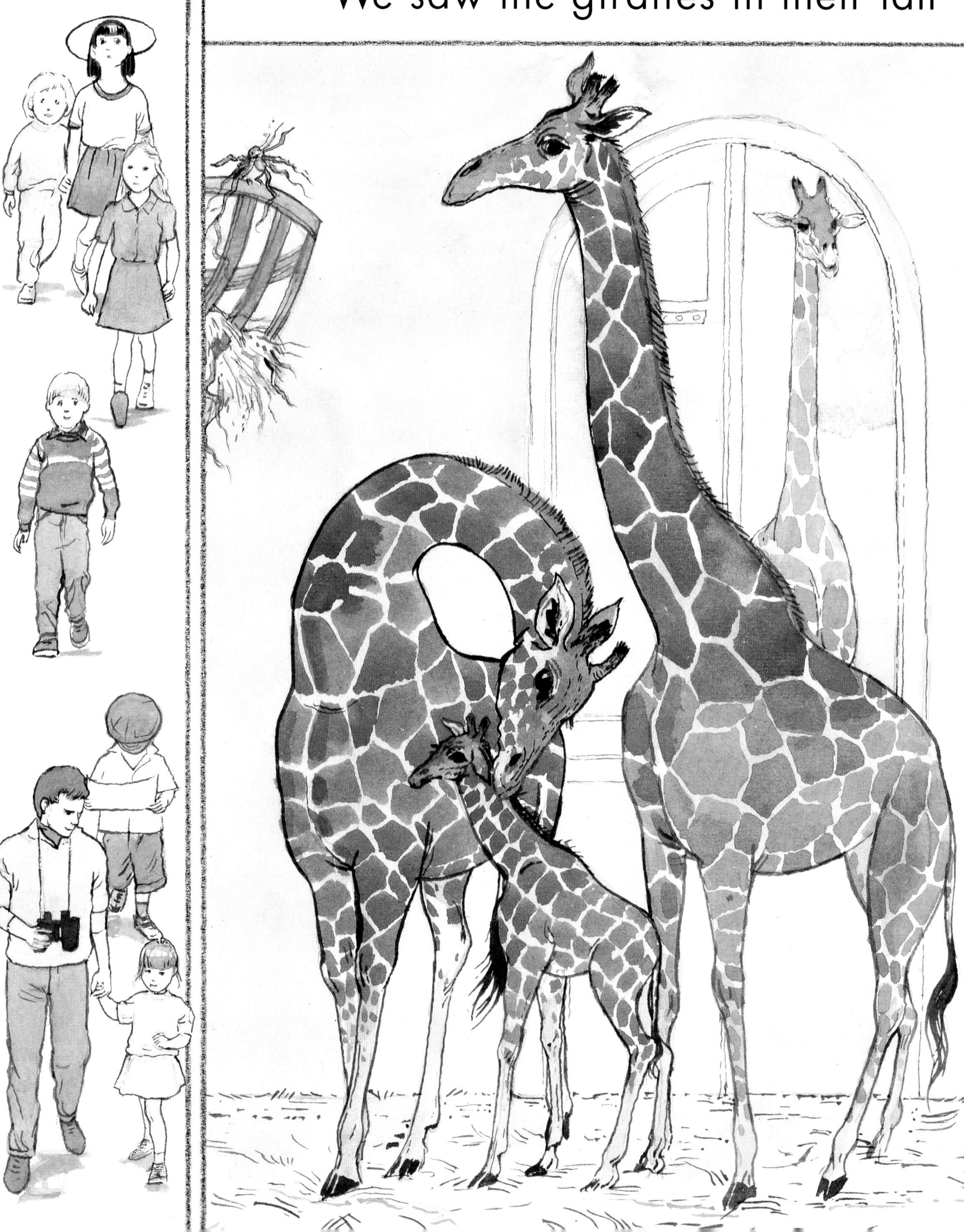

giraffe-house.

Just past the grizzly bear,

we spied the sparrows.

And in the end we liked

that best, spying the sparrows and their nest.

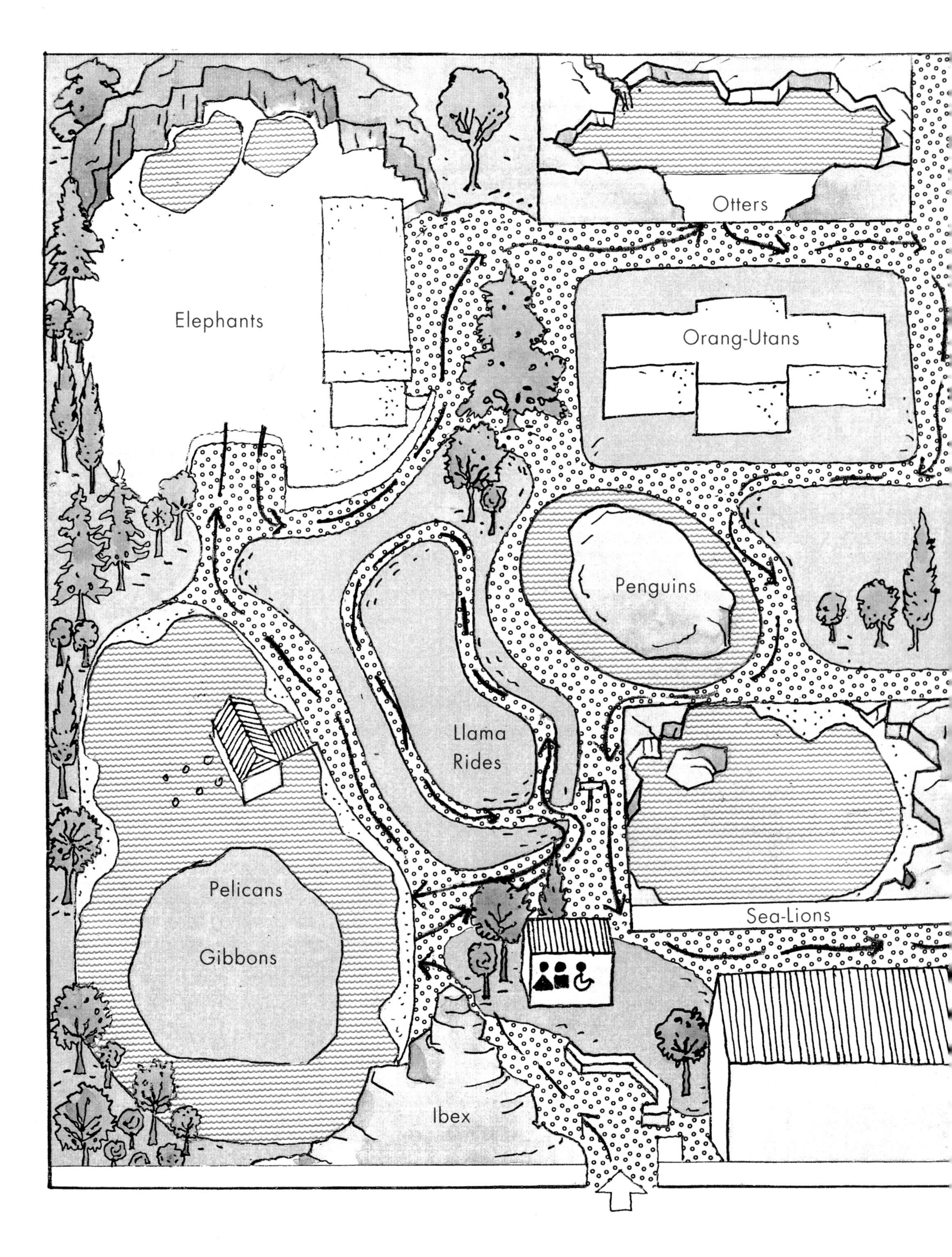
Otters
Elephants
Orang-Utans
Penguins
Llama
Rides
Pelicans
Gibbons
Sea-Lions
Ibex